Real Men Don't Eat Quiche

In true, *Real Man fashion,*
thousands of live trees were
sacrificed in order to make
this book.

Real Men, after all, couldn't
possibly take anything seriously
that was written on recycled paper.

Real Men Don't Eat Quiche

BY BRUCE FEIRSTEIN

Illustrated by Lee Lorenz

PUBLISHED BY POCKET BOOKS NEW YORK

Portions of this originally appeared in *Playboy*.

* * *

This essay is dedicated to Suzanne and Frank Schwartz; a pair of die-hard Real Men.

Additionally, a large measure of thanks is due Jim Morgan of *Playboy*, who shaped and encouraged the original idea; plus Patty Detroit, Marty Asher, Lee Lorenz, Peggy Siegal, Jacques Chazaud, Milton Charles, Trish Todd and Peter Minichiello.

Also, the IBM Displaywriter, serial number 6580-26-00 19972.

Another *Original* publication of POCKET BOOKS

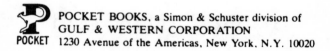

POCKET BOOKS, a Simon & Schuster division of
GULF & WESTERN CORPORATION
1230 Avenue of the Americas, New York, N.Y. 10020

9 8 7 6 5 4 3 2 1

Printed in the U.S.A.

Contents

1
Introduction

"**R**eal men don't eat quiche," said Flex Crush, ordering a breakfast of steak, prime rib, six eggs, and a loaf of toast.

We were sitting in the professional drivers' section of an all-night truckers' pit stop somewhere west of Tulsa on I-44, discussing the plight of men in today's society. Flex, a 225-pound nuclear-waste driver who claims to be one of the last Real Men in existence, was pensive:

"American men are all mixed up today," he began, idly cleaning the 12-gauge shotgun that was sitting across his knees. Off in the distance, the sun was just beginning to rise over the tractor trailers in the parking lot.

"There was a time when this was a nation of Ernest Hemingways. *Real Men*. The kind of guys who could defoliate an entire forest to make a breakfast fire— and then go on to wipe out an endangered species hunting for lunch. But not anymore. We've become a nation of wimps. Pansies. Quiche eaters. Alan Alda types—who cook and clean and *relate* to their wives. Phil Donahue clones—who are *warm* and *sensitive* and *vulnerable*. It's not enough anymore that we earn a living and protect women and children from plagues, famine, and encyclopedia salesmen. But now we're also supposed to be *supportive*. And *understanding*. And *sincere* . . .

"And where's it gotten us? I'll tell you where. Just look around the world today. The Japanese make better cars. The Israelis better soldiers. The Irish better violence. And everybody else is using our embassies for target practice. All things considered, it's no wonder the rest of the world thinks we can't topple a simple banana republic without going to an encounter session about it first.

"I mean, if you really want to see how bad things have gotten, just look at the products America is building today. We used to create things like the Panama Canal. The Hoover Dam. The 'fifty-seven Chevy. The interstate highway system. The front line of the Green Bay Packers. But now? We're building hot-doggers. Electric hair-curlers. FryDaddy. FryBaby. Selecta-Vision. At least the pharaohs built the pyramids. It worries me no end that ten million years from now we'll be remembered as the civilization that created est, frozen yogurt, 'Eight Is Enough,' salad bars, cruise control, restaurants that spin, surf'n'turf, and the 'Phil Donahue Show.' "

The entire restaurant was mesmerized. It was so quiet you could hear the day's fresh-caught fish thawing in the freezer. Flex continued:

"Now, I ask you. Back when America was king—did John Wayne have 'relationships'? Was Clark Gable ever worried about giving his women 'enough space'? Was Bogart ever lonely because he couldn't have a 'meaningful dialogue' with some dame? Do you seriously think we would have ever won World War Two if Ike thought Hitler was just going through a bad mid-life crisis—and should be allowed to 'work it out'?

"Of course not.

"But that's the whole point. If you really want to see what's happening to us, look at today's movies. Instead of having John Wayne fight Nazis and commies for peace and democracy, we've got Dustin Hoffman fighting Meryl Streep for a four-year-old in *Kramer vs. Kramer*. It's no wonder things are so mixed up. Thirty years ago, the Duke would have slapped the broad around and shipped the kid off to military school. But not anymore. I'm convinced things were better off in the past. Men were *men*. Women were sex objects. The rest of the world understood: One false move and we'd nuke 'em."

Flex excused himself from the table to dispense his own brand of justice to several loutish dress designers who were making a ruckus at the far end of the room. But while his desire to return to the "me Tarzan, you Jane" era of interpersonal relationships may be somewhat impractical, he does raise some important questions:

How—in a world where you're expected to be sympathetic, sensitive, and split half the household chores—how do you remain a "Real Man"?

Is it possible to have today's obligatory "relationships" and "shared experiences" and still bowl 300?

Are American men doomed to abandon the principles of Strength, Dignity, and Sylvester Stallone forever?

Or—put in another context—is there a way to acknowledge the existence of the female orgasm and still command the respect of your foreign-auto mechanic?

Hopefully, *Real Men* will shed some light on the answers to these perplexing moral dilemmas—and more.

It's tough! I can never tell when she wants me to be soft and sensitive like Alan Alda or when she wants me to ravage her like a wild boar.

2

The Modern Real Man

*I*n the past, it was easy to be a Real Man. All you had to do was abuse women, steal land from Indians, and find some place to dump the toxic waste.

But not anymore.

Society is much more complex today. We live with different threats and terrors. Robots are challenging us for spots on GM assembly lines. Women are demanding things like equality and respect. And instead of merely having to protect themselves against gunslingers and poker cheats, men today face a far more sinister crowd of predators: IRS agents, uninsured motorists, meter maids, carcinogenic food additives, and electronic banking machines.

So what, then, makes someone a Real Man today?

What sets him apart from the average Joe who can't find his car in the shopping-mall parking lot? Or the joker who takes his girl out on her dream date—only to have the computer reject his credit card at the end of the meal?

How does he prove himself, now that things like barroom brawling, waging war, and baby-seal killing are frowned upon by polite society?

The answer is simple.

A Real Man today is someone who can triumph over the challenges of modern society.

Real Men, for example, do not cower and shake in the face of double-digit inflation.

Real Men do not worry about the diminishing ozone layer.

Real Men are not intimidated by microwave radiation; they're not afraid to fly DC-10s, drive Corvairs, or invest in the city of St. Louis municipal bonds.

In short, strength and bravery are still the hallmark of today's Real Man; but he's just found modern ways to show it.

Real Men carry cash. Never the American Express card.

Real Men don't buy flight insurance.

Real Men don't smoke low-tar cigarettes.

Real Men are not afraid of the communist threat.

Real Men don't take guff from French maître d's.

Real Men don't cry during the "Mary Tyler Moore Show."

Going further, today's Real Man is still interested in the Spartan, simple life. He still believes in "roughing it"; he doesn't own a shower massage, remote-control TV, or an electric blanket.

Real Men don't floss.

Real Men don't use ZIP codes.

Real Men don't have telephones in the shape of Snoopy.

Real Men don't drive Volvos because they're supposedly safer; they don't have special jogging shoes or telephone answering machines. (Real Men, after all, are secure enough to know that if it's important, people will call back.)

Real Men don't itemize their tax deductions.

Real Men still pass in the no-passing lane.

A Real Man would never use a designated hitter.

But this is only the tip of the modern Real Man's psyche.

Today's Real Man is intelligent and astute; he's nobody's fool.

Real Men know that things don't really go better with Coke; he's not really in good hands with Allstate; and weekends were—in fact—not made for Michelob.

Real Men understand that using a Jimmy Connors tennis racquet will not improve a weak backhand; they realize that designer jeans, Paco Rabane and Riunite on ice will not help seduce any woman whose IQ is higher than the average number of a UHF television station.

Basically, today's Real Man is unaffected by fads or fashion.

Real Men don't disco.

Real Men don't eat brunch.

Real Men don't have their hair styled.

Real Men don't meditate, rolf, practice Tai Chi, or use hair thickeners.

Real Men don't advertise in the Personals section of the *Village Voice* for female companionship.

Real Men don't play games with wine in restaurants; they don't sniff the cork and say things like "It's a small, unpretentious, fruity red, with ambitious over-tones of Bordeaux" about a four-dollar bottle of Ripple.

Real Men don't need water beds, lava lights, musk oil, mirrors on the ceiling, X-rated videocassettes, or Ravel's *Bolero*.

Real Men don't want Bo Derek.

Real Men don't use black condoms.

Real Men stop reading—and writing—letters to *Penthouse* when they're sixteen.

Real Men are secure enough to admit they buy *Playboy* for the women.

Politically, Real Men today are, well, realistic.

They don't trust the French.

They don't rely on NATO.

They don't contribute to PBS.

They don't believe in bilingual education.

They don't belong to the National Rifle Association.

And Real Men don't believe in the United Nations.

("After thirty-five years," say Real Men, "all they've proved capable of doing is producing a marginally attractive Christmas card.")

Unlike his predecessors, today's Real Man actually can feel things like sorrow, pity, love, warmth, and sincerity; but he'd never be so vulnerable as to admit them.

All told, today's Real Man is probably closest to Spencer Tracy or Gary Cooper in spirit; he realizes that while birds, flowers, poetry, and small children do not add to the quality of life in quite the same manner as a Super Bowl and six-pack of Bud, he's learned to appreciate them anyway.

But perhaps there's one phrase that sums up his very existence, a simple declaration that he finds symbolic of everything in today's world that's phony, affected, limp, or without merit:

Real Men don't eat quiche.

Admittedly, this may seem—if you'll forgive the pun— a bit hard to swallow at first.

But think about it.

Could John Wayne ever have taken Normandy, Iwo Jima, Korea, the Gulf of Tonkin, and the entire Wild West on a diet of quiche and salad?

3

The Modern Real Man's Credo

Since the beginning of time, men have lived by rules. Moses had his Ten Commandments; King Arthur his Order of the Round Table; Vito Corleone his goon squad for squealers.

Among Real Men, there has always been one simple rule:

Never settle with words what you can accomplish with a flamethrower.

Among today's more enlightened Real Men, this rule still applies—but with one minor modification.

Never settle with words what you can accomplish with a flamethrower—unless the problem in question is a 240-pound halfback for the New York Giants. In which case an apology is always the best policy.

(Given today's violent climate, it's always best to defer to lunatics wielding howitzers, tanks, handguns, or 2,000-pound portable radios. It's a simple fact of life that no matter how tough and strong you are, it all means nothing if you're not alive to show it. This is yet another example of the modern Real Man's newfound intelligence—otherwise known as survival of the smartest.)

Real Man Quiz #1

Q. How many Real Men does it take to cross a river?

A. 5,000. 4,999 to build the suspension bridge, and one to drive across in the tractor trailer.

4

Who's Who in Real Men

*I*t takes a special breed of man to be today's Real Man. You need the honesty of Abe Lincoln, the intelligence of Thomas Jefferson, the integrity of Harry Truman, and the durability of plutonium-90.

So who, you may ask, *are* today's Real Men? Who are our new heroes? Who should we try to emulate? What surefire method can you use to determine the kind of stuff someone is made of?

The answer is simple.

Essentially, the world today can be divided into two categories of men: those who eat quiche, and those who don't. Using this simple acid test, it's possible to immediately determine—without doubt—the mettle of any man.

Jimmy Carter, for example, ate quiche.

George Bush doesn't.

John McEnroe has the guts and determination to be a Real Man; Chevy Chase—child star of *Under the Rainbow, Oh Heavenly Dog, Seems Like Old Times*, and *Modern Problems*—eats quiche.

Elvis Presley was a Real Man, so are Mike Wallace, Morley Safer, Dan Rather, Robert DeNiro, and Pete Rose.

Carol Burnett is a Real Man for taking on the *National Enquirer;* Alan Alda, Dick Van Patten, and Phil Donahue are terminally sincere quiche eaters. No one is really sure about Burt Reynolds.

Frank Sinatra—the Chairman of the Board—does not eat quiche.

James Caan does not eat quiche.

Robert Duvall does not eat quiche.

And neither do Ed Meese, Armand Hammer, Lee Iacocca, Frank Borman, the chairmen of the boards of Mobil, Exxon, Sunoco, U.S. Steel, or any member of the Teamsters Union.

Who else?

Ted Turner does not eat quiche, but Treat Williams certainly does.

Jerry Brown eats quiche on spaceship earth; Don Meredith washes it down with Lipton tea; and Alexander Haig probably munches on it during the periods when he's not "in control here."

Larry Hagman and Paul Newman are both Real Men—but Robert Redford is too sensitive to qualify.

Tommy Lasorda does not eat quiche, but George Steinbrenner has been known to sneak a piece on occasion.

And Billy Martin swears he's off the stuff.

No one on the Supreme Court does anything so trivial as eat quiche.

The National Hockey League is made up entirely of Real Men.

Ed Koch eats quiche—but only because he thinks it might be good for New York City.

No one in Detroit, Minneapolis, Newark, Bangor, or Macon eats the vile dish; but Mick Jagger and Tom Snyder are both suspected of being closet quiche eaters.

And as far as Dick Cavett goes, there's no question:

Real Men don't start three out of every four sentences with the phrase "When Woody Allen and I . . ."

If you're still confused, the following may help.

Real Men

James Garner
Billy Dee Williams
Hughes Rudd
Salvador Allende
Kris Kristofferson
Jane Pauley
John Irving
David Brinkley
Ricardo Montalban
Cesar Romero
Margaret Thatcher
The Hunt Brothers
John Milius
Charles Kuralt
Robert Mitchum
James Galanos
Nancy Reagan

Quiche Eaters

Max Robinson
François Mitterand
Rex Humbard
Jerry Falwell
Robbie Benson
John Davidson
Frank Gifford
Halston (Real Men have two names)
Bianca Jagger
Andy Gibb
Mike Douglas
John Paul II
Jack Klugman

Guys Who Think They're Real Men— But Really Aren't.

Reggie Jackson
Erik Estrada
Deborah Harry
Robert Blake
Geraldo Rivera

Real Man
Quiz #2

Q. How many Real Men does it take to change a light bulb?

A. None. Real Men aren't afraid of the dark.

The
Real Man
Film Festival

Contrary to popular belief, Real Men still go to the movies. First, because it's an integral part of the dating process, and second, because—in the event something is touching—it allows them to cry in the dark.

The problem today, however, is finding movies that appeal to the Real Man's sensibilities—aside from Clint Eastwood extravaganzas, and *Smokey and the Bandit Part 7.*

Real Men, for example, will not pay five dollars to watch Jill Clayburgh try to find herself in *An Unmarried Woman.*

Real Men will not go—for free—to watch Al Pacino try to find himself in *Cruising.*

And there is no amount of money offerable that can coerce a Real Man into seeing *Endless Love, The Blue Lagoon, Moment by Moment, Scenes from a Marriage,* or anything by Antonioni, Zeffirelli, Bergman, Wertmuller, or Truffaut. (As a general rule, Real Men avoid foreign movies like, well, quiche. They believe that the basic idea of film is to see violence and action—not to read subtitles. "And besides," says Flex Crush, "if the movie really had something important to say, they would have made it in English in the first place.")

All this aside, here's a list of the films Real Men will pay hard cash to see.

Spartacus
Patton
Raging Bull
Taxi Driver
Dr. Strangelove
Thunderball
Airport '77
North by Northwest
The Great Escape
High Sierra
The Manchurian Candidate
Red River
Flying Tigers
Rear Window
Where Eagles Dare
Ben Hur
The Warriors
Magnum Force
North Dallas 40

Citizen Kane
Mr. Roberts
The Hustler
The Good, the Bad
    and the Ugly
The French Connection
Deliverance
The Longest Day
Public Enemy
The Godfather
High Noon
Southern Comfort
Mean Streets
The Great Santini
Boys' Town
To Kill a Mockingbird
The Pawnbroker
Love Story

6

How to Turn Yourself into a Modern Gary Cooper

I. The Real Man's Vocabulary

If you're truly going to be a Real Man, you've got to sound like it.

Therefore, keep the following in mind when speaking:

Real Men do not *relate* to anything. They do not have *meaningful dialogues*. They do not talk about *personal space, vibes, karma, bummers,* or *shared experiences.*

A Real Man does not *get behind* anything. They are not trying to get *in touch* with their feelings; they don't care where anybody's *coming from.* And they would surely never say anything like "I'm trying to get my act together."

Further, Real Men do not *do* drugs. They don't *go for it, catch rays, crash, party, boogie, get down,* or *kick out the jams.*

Real Men don't *interact, hyperventilate,* or *obsess;* they don't talk about dieting, raising their consciousness, or trying to work things out.

Real Men do not have mother, father, sister, brother, or inferiority complexes.

Real Men don't *lay raps* on people; they refuse to *go with the flow, repress, O.D., cope,* or have *mid-life crises.*

Real Men do not *mellow out.* They don't talk about opening up more lines of communication with a girl friend.

And Real Men are certainly never *laid back.*

Real Men think; they don't conceptualize. They don't talk about commitments; they never *flash* on anything, or agree with somebody by saying, "I hear you."*

Along similar linguistic lines, Real Men do not *get wasted.* They don't have lovers, shrinks, surrogate parents, or soul-mates. Real Men don't think anything is *neat;* and they never refer to movies as *films.* Or worse—*cinema.*

But perhaps more important than any of this is the fact that Real Men do not talk like Alexander Haig. When a simple yes or no answer is required, you'll get a simple yes or no, and not one of these:

"Well, according to our latest reports, at this point in time, within the usual parameters, allowing for the normal fluctuations and unpredictable variables—and subject to a reassessment in a different time frame—answer-wise, I'd have to respond to your query with a definite guarded affirmative: based on present information, the odds are good that I had quiche for dinner last night."

Among Real Men, this is called Bullshit.

---

*Actually, Real Men find this concept of *hearing somebody* a particularly humorous notion. Given the way high-decibel rock 'n' roll has trashed our hearing during the past two decades, Real Men worry we may well be remembered as the "What?" generation—based on conversations unearthed in discos millions of years from now. Sample interchange: "Hi. Come here often?" "What?" "Haven't I seen you here before?" "What?"

II. The Real Man's Wardrobe

When it comes to personal haberdashery, today's Real Man lives by a simple, although elegant motto: "Never dress like you're trying out for a spot with the Village People."

With this in mind, Real Men don't need the *Dress for Success* books; they understand that satin go-go boots don't make it with a blue suit; and it's best to avoid wearing Indian headgear to the office—simply because the Indians lost the war, and you're likely to be tagged as a loser by association.

Beyond this, there are some specifics:

Real Men don't wear jumpsuits. They don't dress in Italian cyclist uniforms, leather pants, camouflage gear, or anything made of polyester.

Real Men don't wear pith helmets, yachting caps, bikini underwear, Sansabelt slacks, gold chains, pirates' pants, white patent-leather shoes [with matching belts], golf outfits, turquoise jewelry, or anything with more than three zippers.

Real Men who are not cowboys do not wear cowboy boots.

Real Men who aren't Olympic skiers don't wear $5,000 ski outfits.

Real Men who are not Formula-1 race-car drivers do not wear Formula-1 racing team jackets.

And surely, Real Men do not wear T-shirts that say anything as inane as the name of a rock 'n' roll band, their favorite brand of beer, or "I've been to Disneyland."

So what *do* Real Men wear?

Wing tips. Suits and ties. Button-down shirts. And their jeans are designed by a company called Levi-Strauss.

Further, Real Men do not ordinarily wear clothing designed by men with names like Calvin, Geoffrey, Georgio, Yves, Pierre, or Clovis; but if you insist, keep one thing in mind:

Real Men are secure enough to wear their labels *inside* their clothing.

III. The Real Man on Wheels

Remember when being a Real Man meant flying down the highway at 100 mph stone drunk, with one hand on a seventeen-year-old blonde, and the other wrapped around a can of Schlitz?

Fortunately, some things never change—and the automobile still remains the sacred shrine of Real Men everywhere.

But while Real Men still drive too fast, drink too much, and generally reject such obtuse concepts as bridge tolls, fuel economy, environmental controls, and the fifty-five-mile-per-hour speed limit, there *are* several new twists in their rules of the road.

To wit:

1. Real Men no longer drive Corvettes. Despite being able to squander gas with the best of them, even today's least enlightened Real Man finds the notion of a $17,000 plastic car with no trunk somewhat absurd. (Real Men, after all, need cars made of good, solid steel—with enough storage space to carry around wine, women, shotguns, and all the other essential paraphernalia that Real Men find essential on the open road.)

2. Real Men do not drive sports cars—MGs, Fiats, Maseratis, Triumphs, or Aston Martins. They've come to realize that spending a sum equivalent to the gross national debt of England on a car—not to mention having to adopt an auto mechanic—is not the most cost-effective way of proving their masculinity.

3. Real Men do not drive stick shifts. They're secure enough to let their gears be shifted automatically.

4. Real Men—who live in cities—do not drive Jeeps.

5. Real Men don't order the courtesy light group.

6. Real Men do not have vanity plates. (What self-respecting Real Man would drive a car tagged "Cute-sie"? Or "His 'N' Hers"?)

7. Real Men do not put bunny stickers in the rear window; they don't have flared fenders, moon roofs, airdams, fog-lights, racing gloves, cruise control, or six-tone airhorns that play "Here Comes the Bride."

8. Real Men don't own vans with murals of naked women or sunsets painted on the side.

So what do Real Men drive?

It's simple: Chryslers. Massive, hulking, gas-guzzling Chryslers. Indy 500 specials. With four-barrel carburetors, automatic transmissions, and five million cubic inches under the hood.

Real Men, after all, are realistic:

How are you ever going to lose a state trooper in a Honda?

7

*The
Real Man
at Work*

*U*nfortunately, not everyone today can be Red
Adair; there just aren't enough oil-rig fires in
exotic places to go around anymore. And besides—somebody's got to be left to sell cable TV, run
the Pentagon, and fix shoes.

This doesn't mean you can't be a Real Man, however;
the trick is finding the right occupation. Something
that properly reflects the tenets of Strength and Dignity. And the smallest distinctions can make all the
difference in the world.

Jobs held by Real Men
vs.
jobs held by quiche eaters

French chef *vs.* French maître d'
Airline pilot *vs.* Travel agent
Brain surgeon *vs.* Guru
Secretary of Defense *vs.* Secretary of Urban
Development
Garbage man *vs.* Sanitation engineer
President of Lockheed *vs.* President of
the Ford Foundation

Editor of the
Wall Street Journal vs. Editor of *Us*
Fry man in McDonald's *vs.* Fry man in La Crêpe
Appliance salesman *vs.* Consumer advocate
Porn star *vs.* Game show host
Heavyweight Champion Secretary General of
of the world *vs.* the United Nations

You must meet Stan Schofield. He's in a
survival mode too.

Real Man
Quiz #3

Two men are strolling down Fifth Avenue in New York City. Both are dressed in buckskin jackets, cowboy boots, and western shirts. Both are stockbrokers. Both live in Manhattan.

At the corner of Fifty-Seventh Street, one man looks at the other and says: "Say, pardner, why don' we mosey on over to Bloomin'dales and lasso us some quiche 'n cologne?"

Are these Real Men?

8

*The
Real Man's
Library*

Yes, Virginia, today's Real Man *does* read more than *TV Guide, Field & Stream,* and *Gent.*
Along with his stuffed and mounted hunting trophies, here's what you'll find in his library:

Fiction

The Old Man and the Sea, Ernest Hemingway
Lady Chatterly's Lover, D. H. Lawrence
Goldfinger, Ian Fleming
The Shining, Stephen King
Kon-Tiki, Thor Heyerdahl
Tinker, Tailor, Soldier, Spy, John Le Carré
Once Is Not Enough, Jacqueline Susann
The Matarese Circle, Robert Ludlum
Marilyn, Norman Mailer
A Bridge Too Far, Cornelius Ryan
The Dogs of War, Frederick Forsyth
Exodus, Leon Uris
Shogun, James Clavell
The Chapman Report, Irving Wallace
The World According to Garp, John Irving
The Ultra Secret, F. W. Winterbotham
The Story of O, Pauline Reage
The Joy of Sex, Alex Comfort, M.D.
The Warren Report
Roots, Alex Haley

Nonfiction

Future Shock, Alvin Toffler
The Whole Earth Catalog
All the President's Men, Woodward and
   Bernstein
The Rise and Fall of the Third Reich, William
   Shirer
*Clinton's Automotive Guide to the '65 Ford
   LTD*
The Right Stuff, Tom Wolfe
Here's Ed (a biography of Ed McMahon),
   Carroll Carroll
The Making of the President, 1960, Theodore
   H. White
Will, G. Gordon Liddy
The Godfather, Mario Puzo

(In addition, the Real Man's library contains an ex-
tensive collection of L. L. Bean catalogs, a red-bound
edition of *The World Book Encyclopedia* that dates
from grammar school, and—from college—unopened
copies of Samuelson's *Economics,* Gray's *Anatomy,*
and Janson's *History of Art.*

In case you're wondering why he doesn't have a more
contemporary library, the answer is simple: Unlike the
rest of us, Real Men don't join the Book-of-the-Month
Club.)

9

Great Moments in Real Man Literature

"So I put my hand over the flame—just to show
how tough I was."

—G. Gordon Liddy,
writing in his autobiography, *Will*.

10

Three Things You Won't Find in a Real Man's Pockets

1. Lip balm.

2. Breath freshener.

3. Opera tickets.

11
Modern Sex and Romance

Alas, after twenty million years of choosing a mate by knocking her over the head and dragging her home by the hair, even today's most obstinate Real Man has come to realize this is no longer an effective dating technique.

Try as you might, it just doesn't go over well in major metropolitan areas—not to mention there being far better ways to find a mate today, including Club Med, "The Dating Game," and Quaaludes.

Yes, today's Real Man has cleaned up his act.

No more wrestling matches in the backseat of his Buick Riviera. (A sport that Detroit's down-sizing program has made impossible for anyone but midgets, anyway. Can you imagine a Real Man trying to make it in the backseat of a Pinto?)

He no longer uses lines like "It won't go down unless you touch it." Or "If you loved me, you'd do it."

And he's even learned not to be threatened by women who have successful jobs and careers—as long as they don't make as much money as he does.

In short, today's Real Man is charming, enlightened, sensitive, kind, and understanding—at least until he knows a woman long enough to take her for granted. (Say, three weeks.)

Beyond this, here are a few other notes on Real Man sex and romance:

1. Real Men don't like to "do it" on the first date. It makes them feel cheap. And easy.

2. Real Men still discuss the most intimate details of their sex lives with close friends, but they demand absolute silence from female partners. (It's not that there could *possibly* be anything to worry about, but a Real Man expects his girl friends to uphold the sanctity of the bedroom. He won't tolerate discussions of his size, technique, or stamina by former girl friends in the health-club locker room; unless, of course, they confirm his own stories of inhuman prowess.)

3. Real Men are no longer looking for a girl just like Mom—because Mom had no idea about S&M, bondage, wet suits, or some of the more interesting uses for a portable video camera.

4. Real Men are no longer interested in marrying a virgin—because virgins have no idea about S&M, bondage, wet suits, or some of the more interesting uses for a portable video camera.

5. Real Men want women who have *some* sexual experience—but certainly not more than they do.

6. A Real Man today is someone who offers to provide birth control.

7. He's someone who's actually learned to enjoy it on the bottom.

8. Real Men are quieter than most Real Women.

9. Real Men still ask if it was good.

10. Real Men still offer to buy breakfast the next morning.

11. Real Men still send flowers the next day.

12

What Today's Real Man Looks for in a Woman

Personality, intelligence, kindness, a sense of humor, and a good job; sincerity, sympathy, understanding, sweetness, a good sense of doubles tennis—and the ability to fill out an IRS 1040 long form.

Well, goodnight Ralph. It was nice meeting someone so sensitive, aware, and vulnerable. Too bad you're such a wimp.

13

Qualities the Old-Style Real Man Looks for in a Woman

Trust funds. Big breasts.

Real Man
Quiz #4

Q. Why did the Real Man cross the road?

A. It's none of your goddamn business.

14. Great Moments in

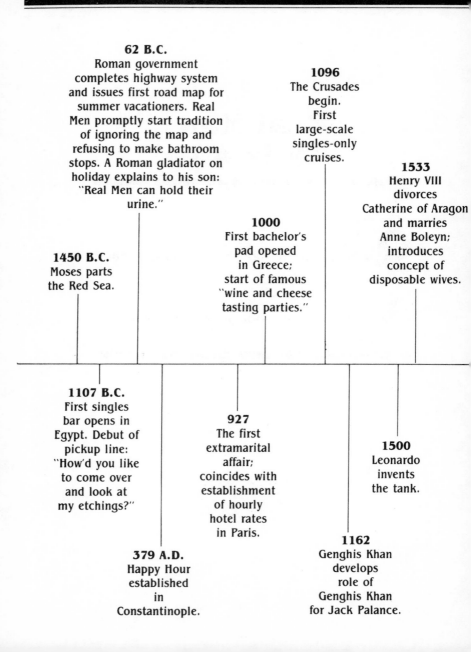

62 B.C.
Roman government completes highway system and issues first road map for summer vacationers. Real Men promptly start tradition of ignoring the map and refusing to make bathroom stops. A Roman gladiator on holiday explains to his son: "Real Men can hold their urine."

1096
The Crusades begin. First large-scale singles-only cruises.

1533
Henry VIII divorces Catherine of Aragon and marries Anne Boleyn; introduces concept of disposable wives.

1000
First bachelor's pad opened in Greece; start of famous "wine and cheese tasting parties."

1450 B.C.
Moses parts the Red Sea.

1107 B.C.
First singles bar opens in Egypt. Debut of pickup line: "How'd you like to come over and look at my etchings?"

927
The first extramarital affair; coincides with establishment of hourly hotel rates in Paris.

1500
Leonardo invents the tank.

1162
Genghis Khan develops role of Genghis Khan for Jack Palance.

379 A.D.
Happy Hour established in Constantinople.

Real Man History

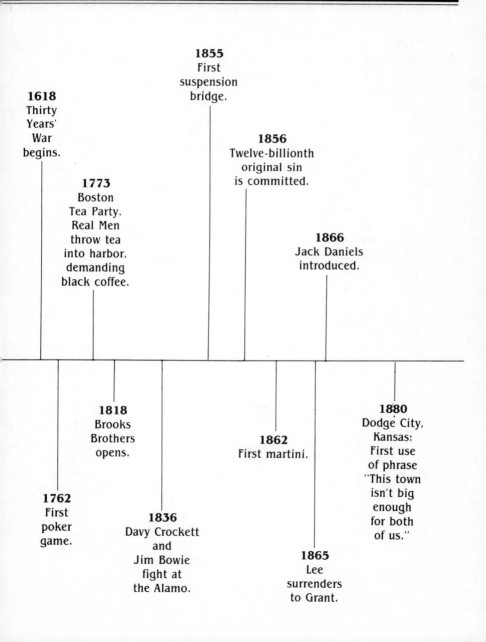

1855
First
suspension
bridge.

1618
Thirty
Years'
War
begins.

1856
Twelve-billionth
original sin
is committed.

1773
Boston
Tea Party.
Real Men
throw tea
into harbor,
demanding
black coffee.

1866
Jack Daniels
introduced.

1818
Brooks
Brothers
opens.

1880
Dodge City,
Kansas:
First use
of phrase
"This town
isn't big
enough
for both
of us."

1862
First martini.

1762
First
poker
game.

1836
Davy Crockett
and
Jim Bowie
fight at
the Alamo.

1865
Lee
surrenders
to Grant.

Great Moments in Real Man History

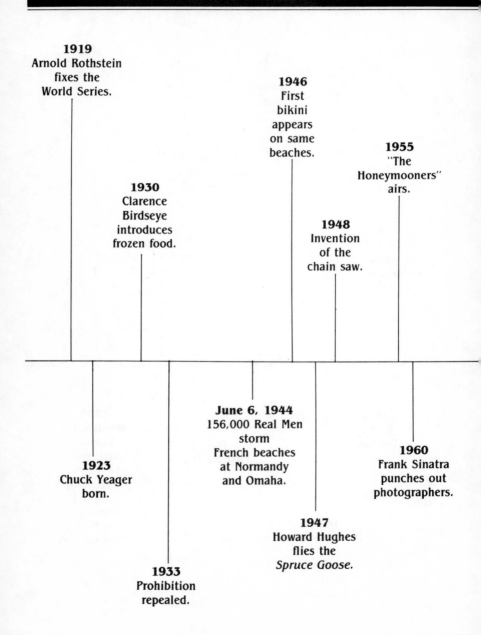

1919
Arnold Rothstein
fixes the
World Series.

1946
First
bikini
appears
on same
beaches.

1955
"The
Honeymooners"
airs.

1930
Clarence
Birdseye
introduces
frozen food.

1948
Invention
of the
chain saw.

1923
Chuck Yeager
born.

June 6, 1944
156,000 Real Men
storm
French beaches
at Normandy
and Omaha.

1960
Frank Sinatra
punches out
photographers.

1947
Howard Hughes
flies the
Spruce Goose.

1933
Prohibition
repealed.

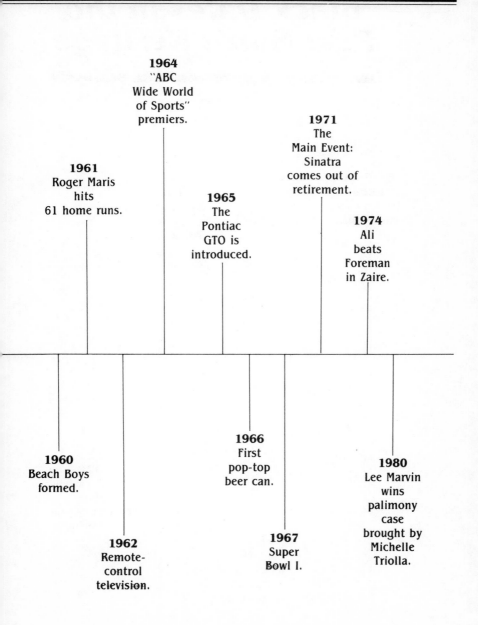

1964
"ABC
Wide World
of Sports"
premiers.

1971
The
Main Event:
Sinatra
comes out of
retirement.

1961
Roger Maris
hits
61 home runs.

1965
The
Pontiac
GTO is
introduced.

1974
Ali
beats
Foreman
in Zaire.

1966
First
pop-top
beer can.

1960
Beach Boys
formed.

1980
Lee Marvin
wins
palimony
case
brought by
Michelle
Triolla.

1962
Remote-
control
television.

1967
Super
Bowl I.

15

Black Dates in the Real Man's Heritage

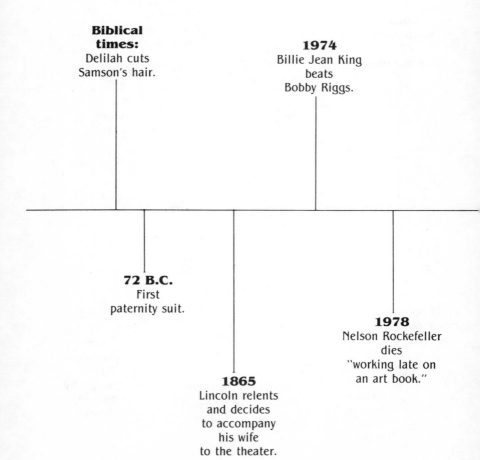

**Biblical
times:**
Delilah cuts
Samson's hair.

1974
Billie Jean King
beats
Bobby Riggs.

72 B.C.
First
paternity suit.

1978
Nelson Rockefeller
dies
"working late on
an art book."

1865
Lincoln relents
and decides
to accompany
his wife
to the theater.

What really knocks me out is calling them "imperialist, blood-sucking swine" and knowing they're picking up the tab for this whole thing.

16

Great Lines from Real Man Movies

"I stick my neck out for nobody."
—Humphrey Bogart in *Casablanca*.

"I love the smell of napalm in the morning."
—Robert Duvall in *Apocalypse Now*.

17

The Old-Style
Real Man in Action

Chicago. February 14th, 1929. Underworld boss
Al Capone orders the St. Valentine's Day ex-
ecution of archrival Bugs Moran.

When Capone is warned it may be necessary
to kill several dozen men in the process, he
replies:

"I'll send flowers."

Oh my God! It's finally happened!

18

Real Men
and Sports

As a rule, Real Men don't play games.

They do, however, participate in organized sports; but as in everything else, the key is choosing the right athletic events—and playing them in the right style.

Or, put more succinctly, a Real Man is someone who can ski through an avalanche—and still manage not to spill any beer.

I. Real Men—
Sanctioned Sports

Real Men hunt big game.
Real Men bust broncos.
Real Men bullfight.
Real Men don't play backgammon, cricket, croquet, curling, squash, handball, or miniature golf.
They don't mud-wrestle.
They don't play Frisbee.
They don't play video games of any nature; they don't windsurf, ride to the hounds, hurtle, run, shoot skeet, or play badminton, archery, squash, polo, or darts.
Real Men participate only in life and death events—where everything is put on the line.
Real Men skydive.
Real Men play ghetto stickball.
Real Men ski jump, mountain climb, shoot the rapids—and sail around the world solo.
Real Men play Monopoly—but only with Real Money.
Real Men don't snorkel or scuba; they go deep-sea diving.
Real Men don't roller-skate; they play Roller Derby.
Real Men don't go fishing; they hunt shark.
Real Men don't get involved with million-dollar international jet-set quiche-eating Formula-I racing; they have demolition derbies.
Real Men don't swim; they dive off cliffs.
They don't balloon; they hang-glide.
They don't figure skate; they speed-skate.
What else?

Real Men pump iron.

Real Men enter tractor-pulling contests—but only against the tractor.

Real Men shot-put for relaxation.

And as far as gambling goes. Real Men don't play black-jack, craps, or slot machines; they play baccarat. (Real Men, you see, idolize James Bond. Their ultimate fantasy is to be sitting in Monte Carlo with Ursula Andress and a million dollars in chips. They long to stare Goldfinger in the eye and say "Banco!" or "Pass me the shoe"—despite having no idea what these phrases mean. The important thing is that they understand no James Bond movie would be complete without them.)

II. Real Men and the Olympics

Every four years, the civilized nations of the world gather to demonstrate their physical prowess on the playing fields.

Real Men, however, take only a passing interest in the competition; their motto is "Why let some low-rent Latin American country shame us on the parallel bars when—given our nuclear superiority—there's really no need for a contest at all?"

Despite this rather jingoistic attitude, American Real Men *do* compete in the Olympics; only they're more careful in choosing the events they participate in.

Real men, for example, don't bobsled.

They don't throw javelins or run relays (Real Men work alone)—and they certainly don't get involved in any sport measured in meters instead of good old American feet.

Ultimately, Real Men compete in only one Olympic event: the decathlon.

The reason for this is simple—and perfectly illustrates the modern Real Man's newfound intelligence.

In 1972, Mark Spitz won five gold medals imitating a dolphin.

In 1976, Bruce Jenner won the decathlon.

Today, Jenner makes millions endorsing everything from Canon cameras to Wheaties.

And where's Spitz? He's a dentist in southern California, drilling teeth at forty dollars a pop.

Real Men, you see, are smart enough to foresee that the future does not belong to the fish.

A final note
on the Olympics

Today, Real Men feel the Olympics are slightly out of date. They question whether contests that test such antiquated skills as running, jumping, or throwing things have any place in the modern automated world.

Thus, they've started a movement to create the "Urban Olympics," complete with events like "the four-mile broken-foreign-car push"; "social climbing"; "800-meter freestyle traffic dodging"; "bus catching"; "bureaucracy hurdling"; "the 3,000-mile cross-country rumor relay"; "the 100-yard mad dash in a thunderstorm with freshly dry-cleaned clothes"; and the "Ghetto Decathlon"—where junkies race against each other to (**1**) break into an apartment, (**2**)terrorize the residents, (**3**) steal their television set, (**4**) run two miles and (**5**) climb a chain-link fence with it, (**6**) find a pawnshop, (**7**) score the dope, (**8**) break into a tenement, (**9**) run up four flights of steps, and, finally (**10**) shoot up.

(The benefits of this contest are twofold: It not only tests the endurance of a nation's dope addicts, but—more important—it gets them off the streets.)

Unfortunately, as of this writing, the U.S. Olympic Committee has yet to recognize the validity of any of these events.

III. It's How You Play the Game That Counts

Naturally, Real Men do participate in baseball, football, basketball, and tennis. But it's the manner in which they play that separates a Real Man from the quiche eaters.

As a basic rule, Real Men don't bunt. They don't sacrifice-fly, foul out, endorse light beer, or settle for ground-rule doubles. Real Men show up for spring training on time; they don't moan and gripe about making a million dollars per season. A Real Man is someone who'd rather strike out than take a base-on-balls. And there's nothing a Real Man likes better than the challenge of sudden-death overtime.

Getting still more specific:

In football, Real Men don't run out the clock. They don't punt; they don't call for a fair catch, or dance after scoring a touchdown. Real Football Players don't take drugs: They *relish* the pain.

A Real Man is someone who can "relate" to the thrill of victory—but can't "get behind" the agony of defeat.

Real Men don't give locker-room interviews.

Real Men don't pour champagne over the coach's head.

Real Men admit it's truly not how you play the game that counts—but how much your option is renewed for.

Real Men don't huddle; they don't smack each other on the ass, hug after winning, or retire to do the play-by-play for NBC.

Real Men who watch sports on television don't need the instant replay.

In basketball, Real Men don't goal-tend. They don't break the backboard. They don't miss foul shots. And surely they don't go for an easy lay-up when there's the possibility of making a three-point play.

In both football and basketball, a Real Man is some-one who plays both offense *and* defense. In the same game.

Real Men don't need to warm up; they don't wrap themselves in Ace bandages. And they never pray be-fore a big game.

The Real Men rules for tennis are slightly different.

Real Men don't use Prince racquets.

They still use *white* balls.

And they don't blame their mistakes on court sur-face, equipment failure, crowd noise, or bizarre ath-letic diseases. A Real Man can win a tennis match in the middle of a race riot; he doesn't say things like "Sorry, but I can only play on grass," "The racquet wasn't strung to eighty-five pounds," or "I used to be ranked, but then my elbow went."

As far as clothing goes, Real Men don't amble onto the court attired in anything but tennis whites. Real men subscribe to tradition; they don't believe in tennis blues, tennis greens, or tennis pinks—and they take great pains to avoid looking like a walking advertise-ment for Adidas, Wilson, Spaulding, Cross-Court, Tre-torn, Prince, or Head. (Real Men don't trust anyone who wears a Head sweatband across his forehead; they figure it doesn't say much for the player's innate in-telligence if he has to label his extremities in this man-ner. They can't help but wonder if his socks say "feet.")

If all this seems confusing, the following may help.

IV. How to Play the Real Man's Game of Tennis

First, grip your racquet firmly. (Remember—Real Men use wood racquets. Only French maître d's use equipment made of steel, aluminum, beryllium, titanium, or quiche.)

Now, take the racquet and tuck it gently, but authoritatively, in the area beneath your shoulderblades known as the underarm. (In case you're not intimately familiar with this spot, it's the place where Real Men sweat.)

Next, with your free hand, reach for the bottle of Heineken you've placed in front of you. Grasp the bottle firmly—as if you're shaking hands with it—and slowly raise it up to your lips. (This is the first important step as far as form is concerned. Make sure you keep your forearm and wrist straight; swing the bottle up from your elbow. You should be prepared to practice this movement until you get it right.)

Holding the bottle at lip height, aim for the sweet spot in the center of your mouth. Anticipation and control are everything here; bend slightly at the knees, stay on the balls of your feet, and smoothly tilt the bottle backward. If you've done this correctly, the beverage should float out of the bottle down the center of your tongue; you should be able to *feel* the shot slide down your throat.

Now comes the critical part: the follow-through. The moment that separates the Richard Widmarks of the tennis set from the Phil Donahue/Alan Alda crowd.

Gently, but firmly, place the bottle back down on the bar—aiming for the same spot you picked it up from in the first place. Be careful to keep your forearm and wrist straight. There's no surer sign of a quiche eater than someone who misses the bar altogether—resulting in broken bottles, smashed egos, and bad form all around.

Once you've perfected this technique (through dozens of practice bottles) you'll be ready to trot onto the court—and whip the pants off your opponent.

Note: In the unlikely event you lose, this technique offers one additional advantage: You'll be too drunk to remember.

19

*Real Men
and Television*

When Vladimir Zworykin invented television in 1923, his goal was far greater than the mere transmission of moving pictures.

He wanted to invent something that would allow Real Men to avoid having to talk to their families after dinner.

And in its early years, television did just that. There were countless hours of Real Men value-confirming sports, violence, and homicides.

But gradually things changed. Left-wingers preached that television could educate and enlighten the masses. They claimed it could advance our culture. And what was once a gold mine for Real Men quickly became a vast wasteland—filled with fluff like Dick Cavett, Donny and Marie, "Family Feud," "Masterpiece Theatre," Mike Douglas, Tony Orlando, the "Barbara Walters Special," and "Little House on the Prairie."

In short, stuff with no guts. Programming that can't possibly hold up to "Gunsmoke," "Rat Patrol," or anything produced by Jack Webb.

Keeping this in mind, it's easy to understand why Real Men have deserted the tube in droves during the past few seasons.

This isn't to say they're lost forever; but it'll take some ingenious programming to get them back.

The Real Man's

	SUNDAY	MONDAY	TUESDAY
Daytime	Football		
7:00	Dragnet	Adam-12	Mod Squad*
7:30	Kojak	Emergency!	The Rifleman
8:00		S.W.A.T.	Highway Patrol
8:30	Mannix	Hawaii Five-O	Supertrain
9:00			
9:30	Gunsmoke	Monday Night Football	TV Movie: *Brian's Song*
10:00			
10:30	Star Trek		
11:00			
11:30	Mission: Impossible	The Tonight Show; Guest Host Burt Reynolds	
12:00			Professional Wrestling
12:30			
1:00			

*Real Men love to hear Linc say "Solid."

Television Utopia

WEDNESDAY	THURSDAY	FRIDAY	SATURDAY
			Baseball
The Untouchables	Combat	Hogan's Heroes	Rat Patrol
Columbo	Rawhide	Twilight Zone	Rockford Files
	Racket Squad	Mannix	
Bonanza	Hill Street Blues		Cannon
		The Fugitive	
Vegas	Sgt. Bilko		Anything starring Robert Vaughn, Lee Majors, or Robert Wagner
		Maverick	
Naked City	The World Series		The Old FBI
		Have Gun Will Travel (Paladin)	
Sports Update			Love Boat
Super Bowl Minutes		Movie: *Viva Las Vegas* (1964), Ann-Margret, Elvis Presley	
Tom Snyder: New Kennedy Assassination Theories and The Clash			Fantasy Island

20

Five Things Today's Real Man Doesn't Do at a Party

1. Get sick.

2. Imitate Steve Martin.

3. Crush beer cans against his forehead.

4. Brawl.

5. Imitate routines from "Saturday Night Live."

21
The Real Man's Nutritional Guide

By now you're probably wondering: If a Real Man doesn't eat quiche, just what does his diet consist of?

Essentially, Real Men are meat and potatoes eaters.

Real Men eat beef.

They eat frozen peas.

And watermelon.

Plus French fries and apple pie. (Two important diet staples.)

As a general rule, Real Men won't eat anything that is poached, sautéed, minced, blended, glazed, curried, flambéed, stir-fried, or en brochette.

Real Men don't eat brie; they prefer presliced, individually wrapped American singles.

Real Men don't start the day with eggs benedict; they eat flapjacks. Or bacon. Or—if possible—roofing nails.

Real Men don't know how to cook; they only know how to thaw.

And—above everything else—all trends aside—Real Men refuse to refer to spaghetti as pasta.

14 Things You Won't Find in a Real Man's Stomach

1. Mussels
2. Pâté
3. Poached salmon
4. Tofu
5. Bean curd
6. Yogurt
7. Asparagus
8. Broccoli
9. Creamed spinach
10. Quail
11. Rice Pilaf
12. Arugola salad
13. Light beer
14. Veal

Admittedly, this list is incomplete: Real Men avoid all members of the wimp food group, including crudités, lemon mousse, crêpes, avocado, capons, chives, shrimp dip, and fruit compote.

This isn't to say that Real Men don't eat well-balanced meals, however:

The Real Man's Diet

Each day, Real Men try to eat something from each of the five critical Real Man food groups:

Protein

Steak
Hamburger
Cheeseburger
Bacon-cheeseburger
California burger
Pizza burger
Chili burger
Big Mac
Whopper
Kentucky Fried Chicken
Ham and swiss on rye*

Liquids

Beer
Imported beer
Imported dark beer
Gatorade
Jack Daniels***

Carbohydrates

Spaghetti
Macaroni and cheese
French fries
Home fries
Hash browns
Potato chips**
Pretzels

Nourishment

Ring Dings
Devil Dogs
Cheez Whiz
Twinkies
Mallomars
Double-stuffed Oreos
Baskin-Robbins pralines and cream

Fruit and Vegetables

Corn on the cob
Orange soda

Notes:

*Ham and swiss on rye is consumed at lunch only.

**Only honest cholesterol-packed potato chips will do; Real Men don't eat Pringles.

***Jack Daniels or black coffee are the only acceptable evening beverages. Real Men are not affected by caffeine; they don't *need* Sanka.
Further, Real Men don't go for gimmick drinks. Where would the world be today if John Wayne had saddled up to the bar in Dodge City and said, "Give me a stiff Piña Colada?"

22

Two Colors That Do Not Appear in the Real Man's Wardrobe

Puce. And mauve.

23

The Real Man and His Music

If you ask ten different Real Men what kind of music they like, you'll probably get ten different answers—not to mention a half dozen fistfights. But they all will agree on at least one thing: There's nothing quite like the sound of the ocean at night, a roaring campfire on the beach, a giggling sixteen-year-old nymphet, and—for atmosphere—the Beach Boys singing "Good Vibrations."

Beyond this piece of musical heaven, here are several other observations:

Real Men do not listen to Art Garfunkel.

Real Men weren't upset when the Beatles broke up; they don't believe Barry Manilow wrote the songs that made the whole world sing; they don't want to sound like the Bee Gees. (Real Men don't sing falsetto.)

Real Men don't get into the mellow sound.

Real Men don't own albums by the Hollywood Strings.

The "Anvil Chorus" is the Real Man's concerto.

Luciano Pavarotti is a Real Man; Burt Bacharach is not. And Bob Dylan definitely eats quiche.

Kenny Loggins, Bread, ABBA, the Carpenters, Air Supply, Queen, and Don McLean are all certified quiche eaters.

Real Men don't buy 45s. They don't buy disco mixes.
And they don't order records late at night from K-Tel. *

A few other musical notes:

Every Real Man owns the following records: "My Way,"
by Frank Sinatra; "I Heard You're Getting Married," the
Brooklyn Bridge; "Tumbling Dice," the Rolling Stones;
"Linda Ronstadt's Greatest Hits"; "Silhouettes," the Rays;
"All I Have to Do Is Dream," the Everly Brothers; "See
You in September," the Four Seasons; "Tell Laura I
Love Her," Ray Peterson; and "Rocky's Theme," by Bill
Conte.

Real Men are not Grateful Dead freaks.

They don't idolize Cher.

They don't listen to Kiss.

And they can't bear Jackson Browne: Real Men find
it hard to sympathize with a millionaire prima donna
rock 'n' roll star who insists on complaining about how
tough his life is on the road.

Similarly, Real Men don't take the political rantings
of Graham Nash, Joan Baez, Grace Slick, or David
Crosby seriously. Real Men find something hypocriti-
cal about pop stars who rail against big business, and
then make millions recording for RCA, CBS, or Warner
Brothers.

In the past, there've been dozens of musicians who
qualify for Real Man status, including Barry Sandler
("Ballad of the Green Berets"), Beethoven, Elvis, Are-
tha Franklin, Cab Calloway, Mario Lanza, Jerry Lee
Lewis, Gary U.S. Bonds, Barry White, and Randy Newman.

---

*Actually, the whole notion of commercials that begin "Do you remember
those fabulous sixties?" bothers Real Men. They worry we've been so busy
remembering the sixties during the seventies and eighties that no one has
bothered to write any new music. Which means that twenty years from now
the commercials will begin: "Hey . . . Do you remember remembering the
sixties in 1982? Now from K-Tel, you can get this . . ." Ordinarily, Real Men
are not afraid of the future—but given the choice of a future filled with this
or quiche—they'd probably opt for the small French pies.

But of everyone in music today, there's probably no one who typifies the modern Real Man better than Bruce Springsteen. He's tough and honest—yet not above admitting he's made of mush inside. He's even—perish the thought—poetic. And here, for the six or seven people in the United States who haven't heard his music yet, is a compilation of every song he's ever written:

*It was summer/down at the beach
The boys had no jobs/the girls
danced till dawn/looking for rich guys.*

*We were driving up the parkway/
Me and the magic rat/When just
in front of us/in the toll booth/
a car overturned.*

*I was drunk/I was busted/I was going
nowhere on the parkway/It's an
eight-lane asphalt path to oblivion.*

*I went over to the car/and there/
in the glass and beer cans/lay a
girl named Sandy.*

*I held Sandy in my arms/plied Sandy
with all my charms/felt nothing but
alarm for her condition.*

She looked up at me and said—

*Bruce—I'm pregnant.
And I work all night/and watch "General
Hospital" during the day/it's a maudlin
existence.*

*I told her, Sandy/I'd love to stay
with you girl/but I've got to go over the
river/through the woods/up the parkway/
through the tunnel/across the bridge.*

*To meet a man on Tenth Avenue/in Jungleland/
who's going to give me a record contract/
and put me on the cover of* Newsweek/and Time.

*And she looked up at me/with those big
Jersey Shore eyes/and said:*

"Bruce, we'll ride together."

24

The Real Man's Résumé

J. WINSTON SMITH III
25 Nails Drive
Wilton, Connecticut
06897

PERSONAL DATA
Birth date: 12/18/32
Health: Excellent
Married

BUSINESS EXPERIENCE

1/73-present	**The Chase Manhattan Bank** 1 Chase Plaza, New York, New York Chief financial officer in charge of denying minorities credit. Other responsibilities include red-lining of marginal neighborhoods, setting usuary interest rates, and abusive currency speculation.
8/71- 12/72	**The Committee to Reelect the President** Washington, D.C. Fund raising and security-related activities.
1/69- 8/71	**The National Security Council** The White House, Washington, D.C. Special assistant to Dr. Kissinger. (The exact nature of this assignment is still classified.)

The Real Man's Résumé

1/64- 1/69	International Telephone and Telegraph La Paz, Bolivia Senior officer in charge of bribes, pay-offs and slush funds.
4/59- 1/64	The Bechtel Corporation Saigon, Vietnam Supervised airport and harbor construction for the U.S. military forces.
8/55- 4/59	The Grumman Corporation Washington, D.C. Lobbyist for advanced weapons systems at the Pentagon.

Military History

7/53- 8/55	Special Services Division, the U.S. Marine Corps Seoul, Korea Enlisted 7/53. Trained at Parris Island and McLean, Virginia. Passed fighter pilot school 8/54.

Education

9/48-
6/53

Yale, New Haven, Connecticut
R.O.T.C.; varsity football. Majored in
history.

Hobbies

Tennis, yachting, polo. Amateur gyne-
cologist.

References

David Rockefeller
The Chase Manhattan Bank
1 Chase Plaza
New York, New York

Henry Kissinger
The River House
New York, New York

Stansfield Turner
c/o The Central Intelligence Agency
McLean, Virginia

Misc.

Married 8/56. Wife's first name is
Muffy; children's names are classified.

Sternwasser here is the Ernest Hemingway of the corporate takeovers.

Quiz: Are You Today's Real Man?

A short quiz for those who still aren't sure.

1. A certain low-rent Persian nation grabs 52 Americans and holds them hostage. Do you **(A)** negotiate; **(B)** send quiche; **(C)** nuke 'em?

2. Phil Donahue is interviewing Alan Alda on channel 2; Dick Cavett is interviewing Woody Allen on channel 4; Geraldo Rivera is interviewing himself on channel 5; and the movie of the week on channel 7 is about a blind eighteen-year-old rape victim who can't decide whether to have the abortion or join the women's professional golf tour. Do you **(A)** go bowling; **(B)** smash the tube; **(C)** send $25 to Jerry Falwell; **(D)** rerun *Deep Throat* on the Betamax?

3. How many pairs of bikini underpants do you own? **(A)** 0; **(B)** 1 (received as a gift); **(C)** more than 1.

4. Your girl friend announces she's having an affair with another woman. Do you **(A)** nuke her; **(B)** send quiche; **(C)** ask if you can watch.

5. How many women have you slept with in the past year? **(A)** 100—300; **(B)** 300—1,000; **(C)** over 1,000.

Scoring: Question 1: Answer **(A)** 5 points; **(B)** 1 point; **(C)** 20 points. Question 2: **(A)** 10; **(B)** 12; **(C)** 0; **(D)** 20. Question 3: **(A)** 15; **(B)** 5; **(C)** 1. Question 4: **(A)** 7; **(B)** 5; **(C)** 15. Question 5: **(A)** 0 (too few); **(B)** 20 (a fine amount); **(C)** 5 (too many; Real men don't believe in cheap sex.)

Interpreting your score: 0—4 points: a certified wimp. 5—10: quiche chef. 10—25: you command respect at intersections. 25 or more: a modern Gary Cooper.

Note: To be honest, the perfect score is 0; Real Men, after all, don't take quizzes in books.

25

The Real Man's Hall of Fame

*E*ach year, the International Brotherhood of Real Men inducts one new member into their prestigious hall of fame. The winner is usually the person who's done the most to promote "Real Manhood" in a world becoming "increasingly overrun with creeps, pansies, and quiche eaters."

Past recipients of the award have included Mickey Mantle, Joe DiMaggio, Albert Schweitzer, Charo, Ed Sullivan, Harry Houdini, Robert Stack, Guy Lombardo, and the Temptations.

And the winner this year?

Francis Ford Coppola. The man who directed the *Godfather* series and *Apocalypse Now.*

A "Fine example of a Real Man" reads the proclamation. "Someone who risks everything for his art, every time. A man who's built his own movie studio and run his own war; a perfect candidate for Secretary of State. If he truly believed in a war and the country went broke, we're sure he'd be willing to personally underwrite the cost for a few days."

No. We are not going to call him Vince Lombardi Joe Montana George Patton Clint Eastwood Punch Press Teddy Roosevelt Abromowitz.

26

A Few Words About Real Women

Real Women don't drive as well as you do.

Real Women have no past—that they tell you about.

Real Women will indulge in your wildest sexual fantasies—and then throw in a few of their own.

Real Women always have orgasms, but say it's only because of you.

Real Women do not believe in palimony.

Real Women can drive a stick shift.

Real Women don't major in sociology.

Real Women grow their own nails.

Real Women shave their legs.

Real Women are louder in bed than most Real Men.

Real Women are not afraid to eat quiche.

27

The Final Advantage to Being Today's Real Man

*I*t's midnight. You and Jacqueline Bisset have just finished dinner in the most elegant restaurant in Paris. The lobster was perfect. The caviar sublime. The waiter has just handed you a check for $324.44.

As you take your final sip of champagne, it's the most anxious moment of the evening. The candles are low. The music, romantic. You gaze deeply into her blue eyes. Her lips purse to kiss you. It's time for the big move.

Gently, you reach across the table and squeeze her hand. Your lips brush across her cheek; you softly coo in her ear:

"Let's split the check."

After all, being a modern Real Man means knowing exactly the right time to be equal.

With me, baby, it's damn the environment—
full speed ahead!